Goldie Blox®

Goldie 🦍 Blox®

GOLDIE BLOX
AND THE THREE DARES

For Abby and Alaina

Library of Congress Cataloging-in-Publication Data
is available upon request.
ISBN 978-0-399-55636-4 (trade) — ISBN 978-0-399-55637-1 (lib. bdg.) —
ISBN 978-0-399-55649-4 (ebook)

randomhousekids.com

Printed in the United States of America
10 9 8 7 6 5 4 3 2 1

This book has been officially leveled by using the
F&P Text Level Gradient™ Leveling System.

x.

GOLDIE BLOX AND THE THREE DARES

Written by Stacy McAnulty
Illustrated by Alan Batson and Grace Mills

Random House 🏠 New York

LIKE TOXIC LAVA

Goldie Blox loved a challenge. Any challenge.

"I bet I could eat three of these," she said, holding up a hot pepper by its stem.

Goldie and her friends were at the Milky Way Diner. Every table in the restaurant was round and painted to look like a planet, the moon, or the sun. The Gearheads, as Goldie called her friends, sat at the sun table. It had room for twelve chairs, and it glowed.

Li Zhang, Goldie's BFFND (best friend from next door), had just bitten into one of the peppers. His face had turned red, then purple, then red again. He gulped down all the drinks on the table.

"Why would you want to eat three hot peppers?" Ruby Rails asked.

"Because I don't want to eat four!" Goldie laughed.

The waitress refilled their water glasses. Li drank all those, too.

"You won't be able to finish even one," Li said. He panted like a dog.

"Watch me," Goldie said. She leaned her head back and opened her mouth.

"I can't look," Val Voltz said. She pulled her hood up to cover her eyes.

Goldie bit off the pepper at the stem. The juice dribbled on her lips. She chewed once.

This isn't so bad, she thought.

She chewed again. Suddenly, it felt like toxic lava was flowing into her mouth.

This is bad. This is really bad, she thought.

Goldie quickly swallowed.

"You don't look so good, Goldie," Ruby said.

"Waitress," Li called out. "We need more water. Please."

Val peeked out from under her hood. "And maybe a fire extinguisher."

The waitress hurried over. Goldie yanked the pitcher of water from her hands and drank. She spilled half of it down the front of her overalls. The Gearheads stared. So did the waitress.

Goldie wiped her mouth with the back of her hand. "One down. Two to go."

"No!" Ruby said. She handed the rest of the

hot peppers to the waitress and ordered ice cream for everyone.

"So, what are we going to do today?" Li asked.

"Wrow roo woo," Goldie said. She was holding an ice cube to her tongue.

"What?" Ruby asked.

Goldie dropped the ice cube into her glass. "Sorry. I have an idea." She reached under the table and pulled out a souped-up skateboard. It had thick wheels, a mini jetpack, cables, and three buttons.

"Epic," Li said.

"What do the buttons do?" Ruby asked.

Goldie pointed to each button. "The green button is the brake. The yellow button is the turbo power. And the red button is a siren."

"Is it safe?" Val asked.

"I won't know until I try it," Goldie said.

4

"Let's go to the skate park."

"Can I try it?" Li asked.

"Sure! You can go second," Goldie replied.

Li's face fell.

"Fine," Goldie said. "Whoever finishes their ice cream first can have the first ride."

The waitress set down four ice cream sundaes. Before Ruby or Val had even picked up their spoons, Goldie and Li had scarfed down their desserts. No spoon necessary. Li lifted his bowl. Goldie's face was covered with whipped cream.

"Done!" they yelled at the same time.

"Val, who won?" Goldie asked. "I was first, right?"

"Don't put me in the middle," Val said.

"I won," Li said. "You didn't finish."

"Yes, I did." Goldie showed Li her empty bowl.

"Um, Goldie," Ruby said. "You have something on your nose."

Goldie reached up to touch her nose. There was a cherry on the end. She laughed. "I guess I didn't finish."

"And I guess I'm riding first," Li said.

"After Val and I finish our ice cream," Ruby corrected him.

Ten minutes later, Goldie and the Gearheads left the Milky Way Diner and headed across the street to the skate park.

"Val, will you record this?" Li asked. "I want it for my website."

"Can I record it without watching?" Val replied.

"I'll do it," Ruby offered.

Goldie handed over her new skateboard. She gave the wheels a spin for good luck.

"What do the buttons do again?" Li asked.

"Green for brake. Yellow for turbo. Red for siren," Goldie said, wishing she was going first.

Li strapped on the helmet and looked into his camera. "This is Li Gravity. Get ready for an epic physics phenom."

He took off for the skateboard course.

"Tell me when it's over," Val said from beneath her hood.

Li started his ride. He skated up and down the ramps, getting serious air at the top of each jump.

"Hey, Goldie," Ruby said. "Why didn't you make the red button stop and the green button turbo? That would make more sense."

"I did. Red for stop. Green for GOOOOO!"

"That's not what you told Li," Val said.

"Oh no!" Goldie reached into her hair, searching for the remote control. She needed to turn off the buttons.

"Li!" Ruby screamed. "Don't press the buttons."

Val dropped her hood and waved frantically.

Li smiled and waved back. He couldn't hear her. Goldie still couldn't find the remote.

"I know it's here somewhere." She shook her head. A screwdriver, a pair of socks, and an unopened candy bar fell to the ground.

Val, Ruby, and Goldie watched as Li pressed

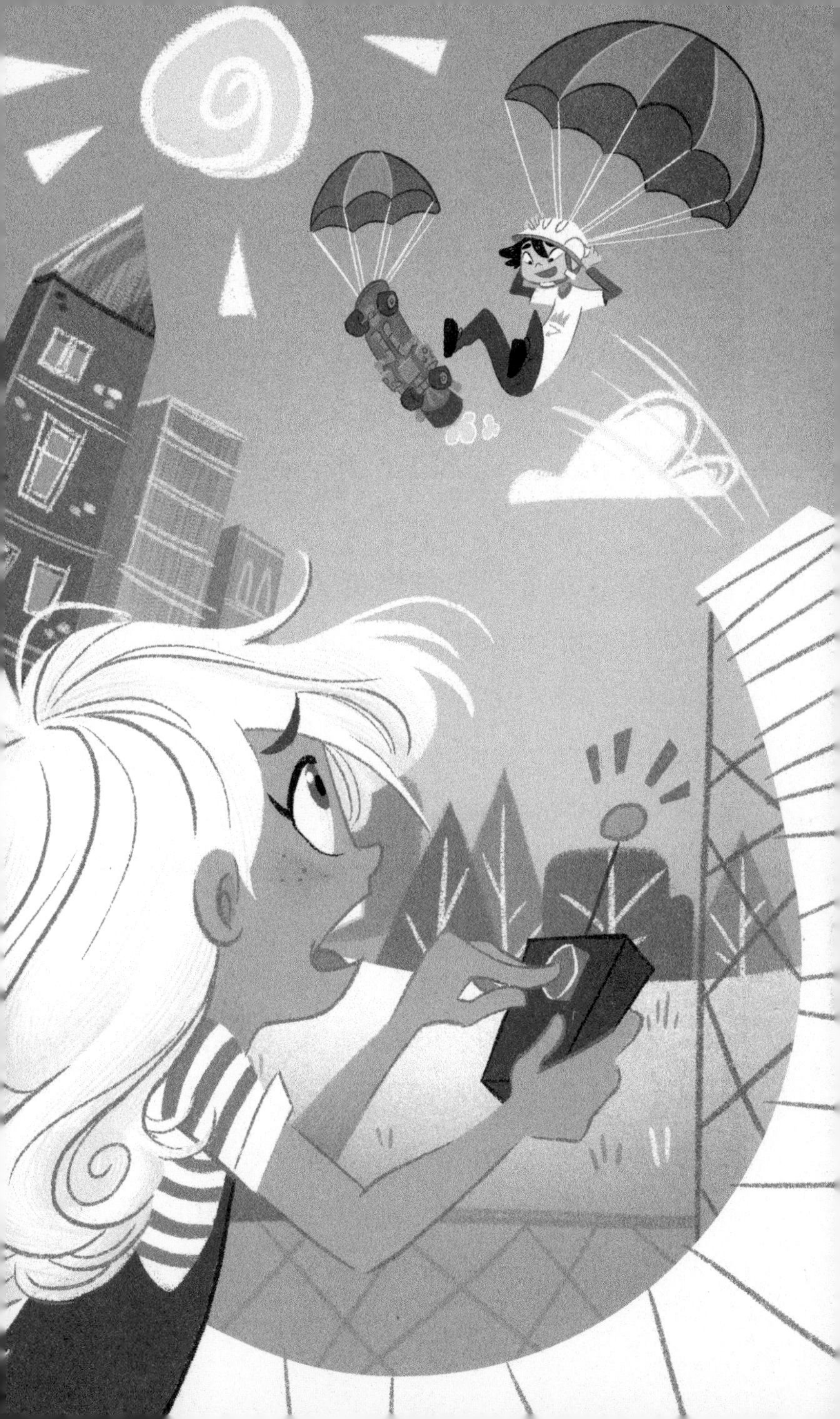

the green button at the end of his ride. Instead of stopping, the skateboard—and Li—shot into the air. They rose higher than the tallest building in Bloxtown!

Val sighed. "We'll never forget you, Li."

Goldie shoved her hand in her pocket. And there it was. The remote!

"I got you, Li!" Goldie shouted. She flicked a switch and turned the knob. Two parachutes deployed, one from the skateboard and the other from Li's helmet. "At least I remembered what these buttons were for."

Li and the skateboard floated across the sky.

Goldie peered up at him. "I hope you're still recording, Rubes. Li will be disappointed if you missed any of this."

"No worries," Ruby replied. "I got it."

"Good," Val said. "Now let's go get Li."

PROPERTY OF BEATRIX BLOX

Nacho, Goldie's friendly basset hound, greeted the Gearheads with doggy kisses when they returned to the BloxShop.

Goldie put the skateboard on a workbench in the middle of the room. This was her favorite place on earth. The BloxShop was an engineering workshop filled with tools and recycled materials. All her best ideas were born here. And most of her not-so-good-ideas, too.

"I just need to rewire the skateboard," she said.

Val peered over Goldie's shoulder. "It looks like you're missing a few wheels."

Goldie frowned. They must have fallen off during the landing. Luckily, Li hadn't broken anything. He'd already watched the video of his skateboarding rocket three times and had posted it to his website.

"Well, if we're fixing the wheels, we should do some other upgrades," Goldie suggested.

"I'd like to add a tracker," Ruby said. "In case you send the skateboard flying to a different continent." She pulled out her minicomputer and tapped on the keyboard.

"G, I've done some quick calculations. I think you can add a bigger jetpack." Li showed her the physics problem he had worked out on the back of a napkin.

"Awesome! There should be one in there." Goldie pointed him toward a pile of spare parts. "And you know what else this board needs?"

"Wheels?" Val repeated.

"Yeah, they're in that pile, too. But also neon lights. That'll make it easier to spot in the sky next time." Goldie knew just where to find some. "I'll be right back."

She slipped through the trapdoor that led to the house. She climbed the rock wall past her bedroom and into the attic. She swung from the rafters to cross the cluttered space.

"There it is." Goldie spotted the box marked NECK PILLOWS AND NEON LIGHTS. Her mom liked to sort things alphabetically.

Goldie flipped open the lid. She chose strings of orange and green, then closed the box back up.

When she turned to leave, a smaller box caught her attention. It was labeled PROPERTY

OF BEATRIX BLOX. Goldie didn't remember seeing that box before.

Gran's stuff? she wondered. *I thought all her things had been donated to the Bloxtown Museum or to charity.*

She laid down the neon lights and lifted Gran's sealed box. *I probably shouldn't open this. At least not without asking.*

Goldie's hesitation lasted only two seconds. She peeled back the tape and carefully lifted the flaps. From what she knew about her grandmother, there was a small chance the box could explode.

It didn't.

Inside was a long red-and-white-striped silk scarf. Goldie recognized it immediately. It was the same scarf Gran was wearing in the picture that hung in their hallway. In the photograph, Gran stood next to an old-fashioned propeller plane. The scarf was wrapped around her neck. She'd just received her pilot's license.

Goldie wrapped the scarf around her own neck. She looked back in the box. The only other item inside was a locked journal. Goldie ran her hand across the cover.

"The Big Book of Blox Dares," she read. The words had been burned into the leather cover. She tried to open it, but the lock held firm. She looked in the box for a key. It was empty.

Luckily, Goldie had a whole shop full of tools. She knew she could pop the lock. She opened a trapdoor in the attic floor and rode the steep slide to the BloxShop and her friends.

"Oh, Goldie, I love the scarf," Ruby said. "Is it vintage?"

Goldie nodded. "If that means old, yes."

"Did you find the lights?" Li asked.

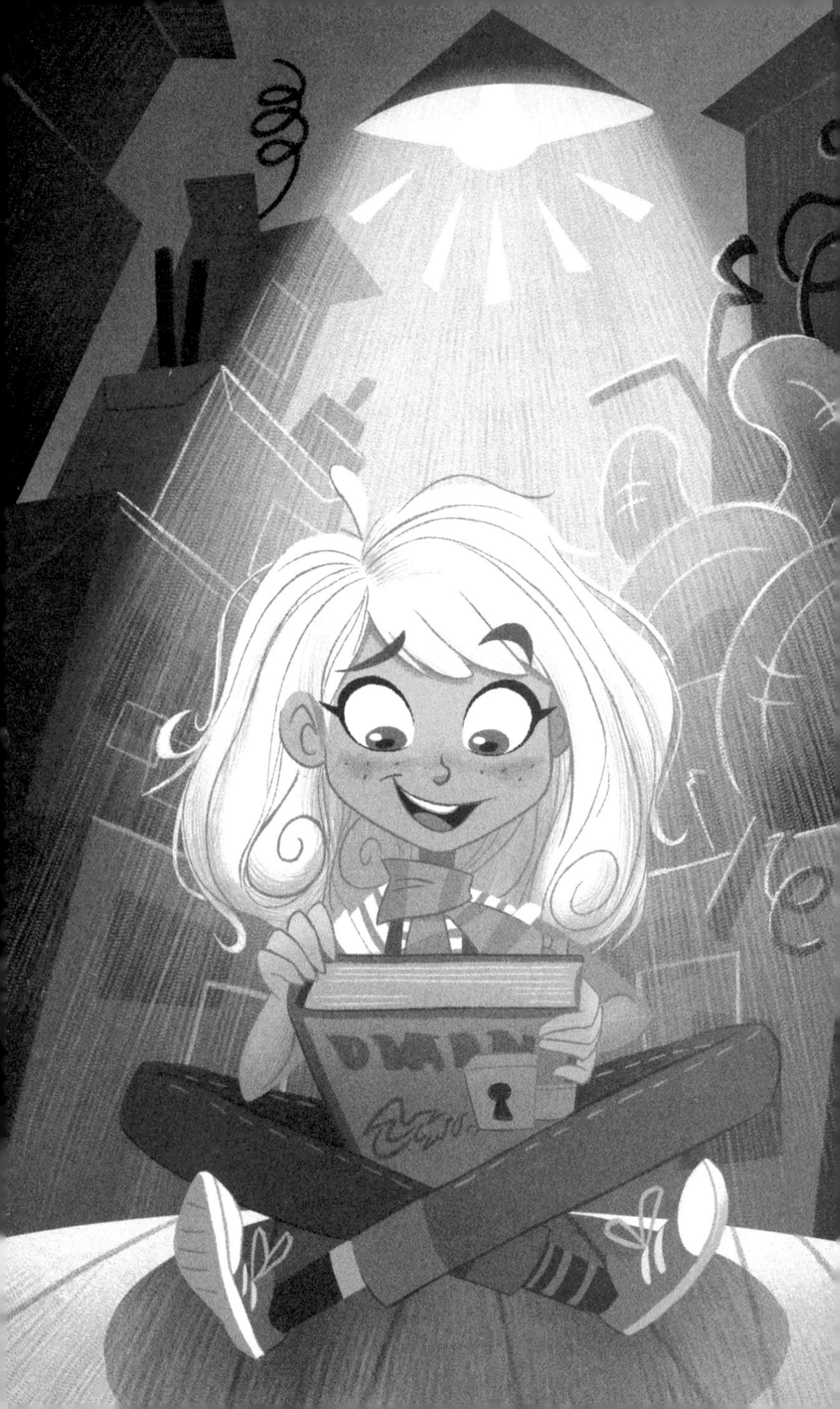

"What?" Goldie had forgotten why she'd gone to the attic in the first place. "Never mind the lights. Or the skateboard. Gearheads, you gotta see this." She held the book out.

"What is it?" Ruby asked. "Looks like a diary."

Val read the cover: *The Big Book of Blox Dares*. She shook her head. "This sounds like trouble. I'd better find the first-aid kit."

"G, what's inside?" Li asked.

"I don't know. I gotta get it open. I need a file . . . maybe some pliers. If that doesn't work, I've got the saw and the blowtorch."

"A blowtorch near paper pages? Not a good idea, Goldie." Ruby put a hand on Goldie's shoulder.

Before Goldie could touch any tools, her mom appeared.

"Hey, gang, who can stay for dinner?" Junie

Blox asked. "Goldie's dad is making bacon waffle enchiladas."

"Yum! Count me in, Mrs. B," Li said.

But Goldie's mom wasn't listening. She had spotted Grandma Beatrix's book. "Where did you find that?" she asked Goldie.

"The attic," Goldie replied.

"I haven't seen this in years." She held out her hands, and Goldie gave her the book. "Your grandmother began this list when she was just a kid. It started simple and small. Like eating a super-hot pepper."

Goldie gasped.

"She kept checking items off the list, and she kept adding to it. I think she almost got all the way to one hundred." Her mom ran a finger over the lock. "Have you opened it?"

"No, I don't have the key," Goldie said. "But I can engineer that."

"And we have this." Li held up a power drill.

"How did I not know about this?" Goldie asked.

Her mom sighed. "Your dad and I hid it. For safety reasons. You've never met a challenge you didn't love."

"That's true," Val said. "I once saw you try to stay underwater longer than a fish."

"I would have won if I had gills," Goldie said. After losing to the guppy, she had invented a mini breathing tank that was perfect to use in the lake.

"Dad and I were going to share it with you eventually. I was thinking around your fiftieth birthday." Goldie's mom winked.

A horn blew, and her dad's voice echoed over the BloxShop intercom. "Chow's on. Come and get it!"

The Gearheads stayed for dinner. They squished around the kitchen table. Goldie's dad had made enough bacon waffle enchiladas for the entire town.

Goldie set the book on the corner of the table.

"Did you see what your daughter found?" Goldie's mom elbowed her husband.

"Isn't that my mother's book? *The Big Book of Blox Dares*?" Goldie's dad had a funny look. Like he couldn't decide whether to laugh or cry.

"I found it in the attic." Goldie gave it to her dad. He held it to his nose and took a giant whiff.

"I have fond memories of this book. My mom—your grandmother—and I finished numbers seventy-one to eighty-four together."

"Mrs. B told us there are one hundred dares

in there," Li said between bites.

"Only fourteen dares for me. But still, those are some of my favorite memories with my mother. I remember rafting down the Rocky River. Walking a tightrope. Building a model of the great pyramids out of breakfast cereal and eating it all in one morning. Good times."

"Do you have the key, Dad?"

"No. I haven't seen it since your Gran was alive. That was before you were born."

I wish I could have met her, Goldie thought. She ran her hand over the red-and-white silk scarf.

"May I see the book, please?" Ruby asked. She used her minicomputer to search for a matching lock and key online.

"Did Grandma B finish all the dares?" Li asked. "She sounds like a woman who got stuff done. I mean, she did start this town, right?"

Goldie's mom laughed. "You guys would have loved her. She did get stuff done. She founded Bloxtown. She built this house with her own two hands."

"With the help of some power tools," Goldie's dad added.

"I can't find a matching key," Ruby said. She closed her minicomputer and handed the book to Val.

Val tried to pry open the lock with a fork. Then Li tried with a butter knife.

"But to answer your question, Li, Beatrix did not finish all the dares. I believe she had three left," Goldie's mom said.

"She always said she'd finish them by her seventy-seventh birthday," her dad said. "She thought seven was a lucky number. She even knew how she was going to celebrate."

"How?" asked Goldie.

"With a stack of lime-chocolate-fig waffles," her dad answered. "She even made the waffles and put them in the freezer. They're still there."

Goldie shot out of her chair. "Wait, you mean there are waffles in our freezer and I've never seen them before?"

"That's because I hid them in a box and labeled it STEAMED BROCCOLI," her mom explained.

Goldie had wondered why they'd never eaten the steamed broccoli. But she'd been too afraid to ask.

Ruby held a napkin to her mouth and gagged. "Twenty-year-old waffles? Ugh."

"Fourteen years," Goldie's dad corrected her. "And they've been vacuum sealed, wrapped in plastic, and kept frozen. Mostly."

Goldie had been hearing about how

delicious Gran's lime-chocolate-fig waffles were since she started eating solid food.

After Li gave up on the lock, he handed the book back to Goldie. "I'm going to finish these dares," Goldie announced.

"Don't you want to see what they are first?" Val asked.

"And I'm going to do them before what would have been Gran's seventy-seventh birthday."

"Do you even know when that is?" Val asked.

"Actually, it's in three days," her dad said.

Her mom raised an eyebrow. "That's convenient. The book of dares shows up just days before the deadline."

"You've got her determination," Goldie's dad told her. "I know you can do it."

"As long as they're not too dangerous," her mom said, wringing her napkin.

"I'm going to finish them," Goldie insisted. "And then I'm going to eat Gran's waffles." She raised her arms triumphantly over her head.

"Eating fourteen-year-old waffles sounds like dare number one hundred and one." Ruby shuddered. "And the grossest dare ever."

A PICKING MACHINE

Goldie and the Gearheads brought the book back to the BloxShop. Li plugged in the power drill.

"Let's open this thing!" he yelled over the sound of the motor.

"Definitely, but we don't need that," Goldie said. "I forgot that I have a picking machine."

"Your *nose*-picking machine?" Val asked.

"No, lock-picking." The machine was an old electric mixer fitted with twenty pointy sticks. Each had a slightly different curve. Goldie clamped the book to her workbench and fired up the lock pick. It was even louder than the power drill. The first pointy stick didn't work. Neither did the second, or the third . . . but the seventeenth pick did. With a groan, the lock popped open.

"Yes!" Goldie pumped her fists in the air. "Now I'm going to finish these dares before Gran's seventy-seventh birthday. Will you guys help me?"

"You know it, G," Li said.

"I'm there for ya," Ruby said.

They all turned and looked at Val.

"Doesn't anyone want to know what the dares are first?" she asked.

"Let's find out." Goldie turned to the

opening page. As expected, all the dares were crossed off. She flipped through the book. Gran's handwriting had changed from sloppy little-kid writing to sloppy adult writing. Still, they were all checked off until the bottom of the last page.

The Gearheads read the final dares.

98. Smell the Rotting Fish Flower
99. Steal the Original Bloxtown Blueprints
100. Have a Picnic on the Moon

Val breathed a sigh of relief and pointed to the last one. "That's impossible. I guess we won't be doing these. We can go back to inventing dangerous skateboards."

"Nothing's impossible," Goldie said.

"You say nothing's impossible?" Val shook her head. "What about teaching a lion to sing?

Or staying awake for an entire year? Or lifting a thousand pounds? Or walking on your hair? Or flying?"

"I flew this morning," Li said proudly.

"And I flew in an airplane last summer when I went to visit my grandmother in Detroit," Ruby said.

"That's not what I meant," Val mumbled.

Goldie put an arm around Val's shoulder. "We can do this, Val. I know it. But we need your help."

Val nodded. "Let's give it a try."

"Okay, Gearheads. We've got three days to get these dares done." Goldie grabbed a dry-erase marker and stood in front of the whiteboard.

Ruby tapped on her minicomputer. "The Rotting Fish Flower grows only at high altitudes," she read from the Internet. "*And* it only blooms once every five years."

"Is it in bloom this year?" Goldie asked.

"Yes. The petals open at dawn every morning for the entire spring."

"Where can we find these flowers?" Goldie asked.

"Please say at our Bloxtown florist," Val added.

"We should be able to find it on top of Rocky Point," Ruby said. She tapped away some more on her minicomputer. "And sorry, Val, the florist does not carry the Rotting Fish Flower."

"This dare doesn't sound very dangerous," Li said.

"That'll make my mom happy," Goldie said.

"Well, that depends," Ruby said. "According to this website, there's a legend that the first person to smell the Rotting Fish Flower fell into a coma. He didn't wake for seven days."

"That can't be true," Val said, worried. "Right?"

"We'll only take a little whiff. I'm sure we'll be fine." Goldie wrote the information on the whiteboard. "What about number ninety-nine? The blueprints?"

"I know where those are," Li said. "I've seen them in the Bloxtown Museum."

"That's right!" Goldie exclaimed. "They keep them rolled up and in a tube. My grandmother created those blueprints. It says so on the sign."

"Why did she want to steal them?" Ruby asked.

"I bet the museum was playing finders keepers, losers weepers," Li said. "The museum likes to say no. I asked to borrow a medieval catapult once. They said no. I only needed it

for like an hour."

Goldie laughed and thought back to third grade. "The one we created worked just as well."

"Goldie," Ruby interrupted. "I don't want to be a thief. Prison attire won't look good on me. I don't like stripes."

"Think of it as borrowing, not stealing. After we get a look at the blueprints, and maybe make a copy, we'll send them back. I'm dying to know what Gran had planned for Bloxtown."

Goldie wrote the details about the blueprints on the whiteboard. "A little tricky but totally doable."

"That just leaves a picnic on the moon,"

Val said.

"Which isn't impossible," Goldie said quickly.

"Yeah, if you're a trained astronaut," Val added.

"I'll figure something out." Goldie drew a picture of a rocket and the moon. "I'm not going to let Gran down."

"And we're not going to let you down, Goldie," Ruby said. "Right, Val?"

Val shrugged. "I guess."

"Get your camping stuff, Gearheads. We're heading to Rocky Point in the morning," Goldie said.

"Wait, camping?" Val jumped up. "I love camping!"

ONE HUNDRED BOTTLES OF SUPERGLUE

Goldie gathered all the normal camping gear—a tent, sleeping bags, and bug spray. She also packed some of her inventions.

Li's grandfather drove the Gearheads to the base of the trail. "I wish I could go with you," he said. "But these knees aren't made for a five-mile hike uphill."

"I wish you could come, too, Mr. Zhang," Goldie said. Li's grandfather told the best stories and never lectured Goldie to be more careful, not even that time when she'd broken one of his handmade clocks.

"I remember your grandmother fondly," he said. "She was a firecracker. I actually helped her with one dare myself."

"Really?" said Goldie.

"Number forty-two. Racing go-carts through Bloxtown. It was a five-hundred-lap challenge."

"Wow!" Goldie was impressed.

"She won, of course. But only by inches. She was a competitor." Mr. Zhang chuckled at the memory.

Goldie smiled. She loved how exciting her gran had been.

"You best get moving," Mr. Zhang said. He pointed at the dog. "Nacho, you're in charge."

"Thanks for the lift, Grandpa." Li gave him a high five.

The Gearheads unloaded the trunk, and

Mr. Zhang drove off. Li and Val each had one normal-sized backpack, Goldie had one overstuffed pack, and Ruby had two large rolling suitcases.

"Have you ever been camping?" Val asked Ruby.

"Like outside in the woods? No. I have slept in my cousin's basement before. In a sleeping bag." Ruby forced a smile. "But that was five years ago."

"What's in the suitcases?" Li asked. "We're only camping for one night."

"I know," Ruby said. "Clothes, shoes, books, towels, sheets, pillows, a portable fan, a lantern, tablecloth, satellite dish—"

"Whoa!" Li held up his hand. "You're not going to need all that."

"Let's help her repack and get it down to just one bag," Goldie suggested. They moved all Ruby's necessary items into a single suitcase and then stashed the other behind a boulder.

"Goldie, your pack looks heavy, too," Val said. "You're sure you don't need to lighten your load?"

"Everything I brought is one hundred percent necessary. And it's not that heavy because of this." Goldie yanked a strap and a giant balloon ejected from her pack. "See? This helps take half the weight."

"Let's get going," Li said.

Val pulled out a map. "We've got a long trip."

"Lead the way." Goldie took out her modified walking stick. It sang as they hiked.

"One hundred bottles of superglue
in the shop.
One hundred bottles of superglue.
Take one down, use it all up.

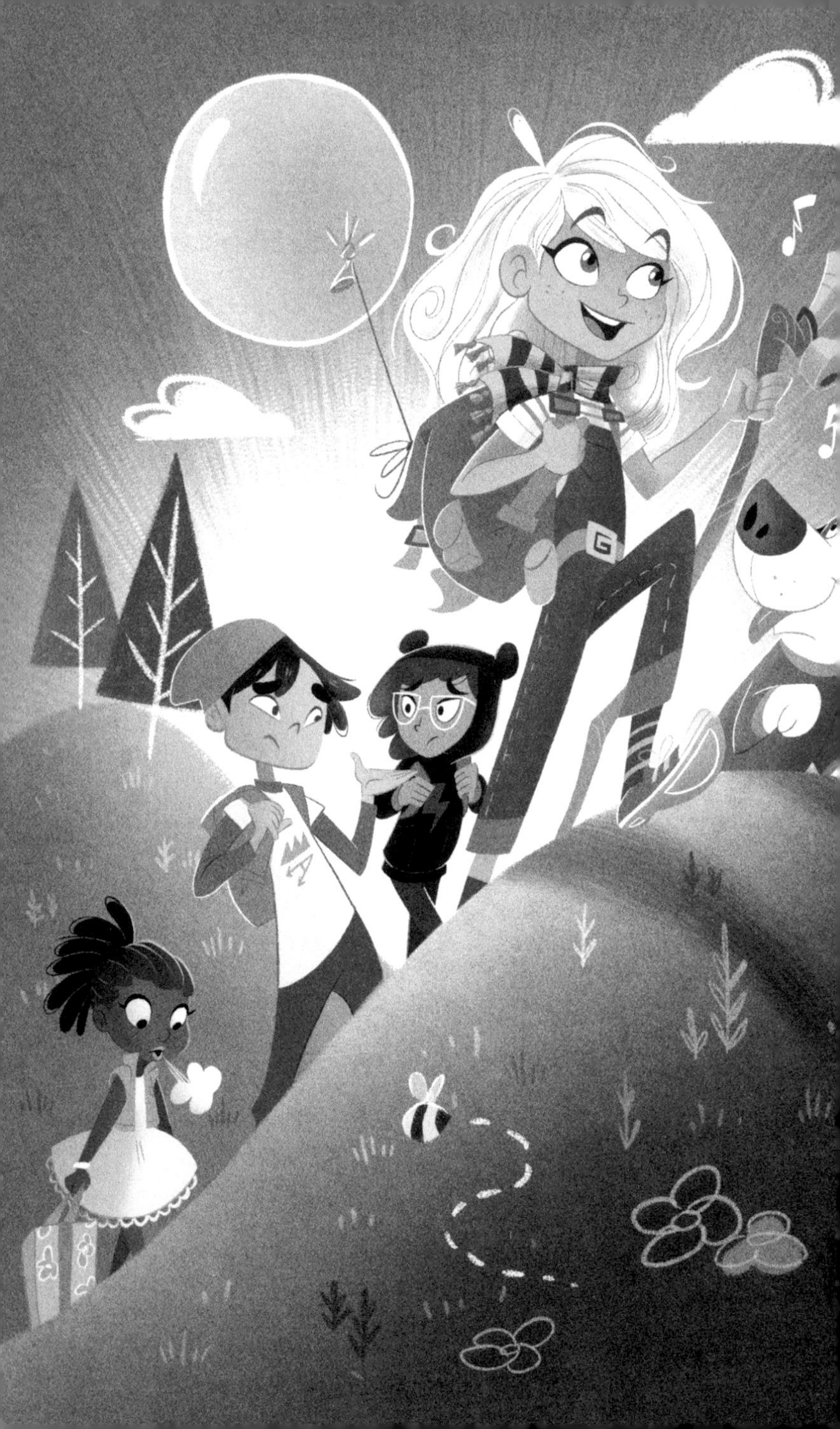

Ninety-nine bottles of superglue

in the shop."

"Did you invent that just to drive us crazy?" Ruby asked.

"Of course not," Goldie said. "You need to make noise when you hike in the woods. You want to let the bears and wolves know you're coming."

"Bears and wolves?" Ruby asked. "Out here?"

"They don't just live in zoos," Val said.

"Don't worry. We've got Nacho." Goldie turned to her dog. Nacho wagged his tail happily.

The walking stick was on its third round of "One Hundred Bottles of Superglue" when the gang came to a stream.

"There should be a bridge here," Val said, looking at the map.

"Maybe it got washed away," Ruby said. "Maybe we need to turn around." She swatted at a bug.

"The water doesn't look too deep," Li said. "Only a foot or two." He borrowed Goldie's walking stick to measure the depth. It went into the water all the way to the handle. The electronics got wet. A spark shot out, and the stick went quiet.

"Sorry, G."

"That's okay. I can fix it, and I'll make it waterproof." Goldie wrote in her notebook.

"And maybe change the song," Ruby suggested.

Val held out the map. "The next bridge is three miles upstream. If it's even there."

"That's too far. We wouldn't get to our campsite until dark." Goldie dug through her pack.

Li started climbing a tree and said, "I think I can jump it."

"I don't think so," Ruby said, putting her hands on her hips. "We need a better way to cross."

"I can engineer that." Goldie pulled a grappling hook launcher from her pack. She hoisted it to her shoulder and shot the hook across the rushing stream. It snagged a tree branch.

"Nice work, G." Li took the end of the rope and tied it to a tree trunk.

"We're going to walk across that tightrope?" Val asked.

"It's not a tightrope. It's a zip line." Goldie took out four harnesses and pulleys. She went first with her backpack and balloon. Then Nacho and Li. Ruby followed them, clutching her suitcase. Val was last.

"You all made it look easy," Val said.

"It is," Goldie said. "And fun."

Val pushed off from the shore with her eyelids closed tight.

"Open your eyes!" Li yelled.

She did. And instantly, Val's worried expression turned into one of glee.

"Wheeeeee!"

Goldie helped Val out of the harness.

"Can we do that again?" Val asked.

"Sure," Goldie answered, "on the way back."

They continued to hike. Because the walking stick was broken, they sang as they went.

The path curved, going higher and higher. Ruby lugged her suitcase. When the suitcase started rolling back down the hill, she chased after it. She tore her pants on a pricker bush.

A mile later, a rockslide covered the trail. The Gearheads had to scramble over rocks and down trees. Val's hand slipped on some moss, and her glasses fell into a crevice.

"No worries, Val. I can get them." Goldie pulled a plunger from her pack. It had a telescoping handle that could extend twenty feet. The plunger suctioned onto the glasses and Goldie pulled them out. But one lens was missing and the other was cracked.

"Thanks anyway," Val said.

"Hey, Gearheads. I gotta use the boys' room." Li pointed behind some pine trees. "I'll be right back."

"There's a bathroom back there?" Ruby asked.

"Not the kind with a door," Goldie explained.

Goldie, Val, Ruby, and Nacho sat on a log and waited for Li. They waited and waited.

"Li! You almost done?" Goldie called.

There was no reply.

"Maybe we should look for him," Val suggested.

"I got this," Ruby said. She opened her minicomputer and took out a small satellite dish. "I put a tracking sticker on everyone." A second later, she'd located Li on her screen.

"There!" Goldie pointed. Li had managed to get behind them and was heading in the wrong direction. The girls ran down the path to stop him. Ruby guided them the whole way.

"Li!" Goldie yelled when she saw the back of his shirt. "Where are you going?"

"Hey, G." He pulled his cap off and scratched his head. "I wasn't lost. I was taking the scenic route."

"The scenic route is in the wrong direction," Val said. She was facing a tree instead of Li because she couldn't see without her glasses.

"We're almost to the campsite," Goldie said. "After we set up and have dinner, we'll have s'mores." She knew the Gearheads were tired. But s'mores made everything better.

Nacho barked in agreement. He was covered in mud, leaves, and feathers.

There was no more singing as they hiked

for another hour. When they got to the campsite clearing, they set up their tent. Li gathered firewood. Ruby made certain the tent was bug- and debris-free. Val checked and rechecked the map to make sure they were on the right path.

Over the campfire, Goldie made Blox stew.

"What's in it?" Ruby asked.

"You should ask what's *not* in it." Goldie poured in cans of corn, beans, sausage, artichokes, and pineapple, and a box that didn't have a label.

"I'm starving," Li said. "I could eat anything."

"You're about to," Val warned.

All the hiking had made them

hungry. They each ate two bowls. Then they had s'mores and turned in for the night.

Goldie zipped the tent closed. "Goodnight, Gearheads. Thanks for coming on this adventure with me. Tomorrow, we will find the Rotting Fish Flower, completing one of Gran's dares."

Goldie fell asleep and dreamed about the gran she'd never met. She smiled in her sleep—until a loud *CRUNCH* woke them all up.

SASQUATCH

"What was that?" Ruby whispered. "Was it a mountain lion?"

They were all awake. Goldie turned on her flashlight.

"There have been cougars spotted in this area," Val answered.

"It didn't sound like a cougar to me," Goldie said. "It's probably nothing." They all strained their ears, listening. Nacho hid under a sleeping bag.

Twigs snapped outside the tent. Something

grunted. Ruby joined Nacho under the sleeping bag.

"It's a Sasquatch!" Li declared. "Where's my video camera?"

"Let's check it out." Goldie unzipped the tent.

"I'll stay here and keep Nacho company," Ruby said, shaking. "He seems scared."

Goldie turned off her flashlight so she wouldn't scare the cougar or Sasquatch. Val and Li followed her out of the tent.

The creature was moving away from their camp. The rustling came from farther up the mountain.

"Come on," Goldie whispered. "It's getting away."

"Isn't that a good thing?" Val asked. But Li and Goldie were already running up the path.

As they got closer, they realized that there

was more than one creature ahead of them.

Goldie and Li crouched behind a blackberry bush.

Val caught up. "Bears!" she gasped.

"Not bears," Goldie said. "Humans."

"I can't see much with my broken glasses," Val explained. "To me, they look fuzzy. Like bears."

"To me, they look like scientists," Li said. He pointed to the tent they were putting up. BOTANICAL RESEARCH INSTITUTE was printed on the side.

"Camping scientists. Kinda like us." Goldie stood up. "Maybe we should introduce ourselves."

"Maybe we should get back to Ruby and Nacho," Val suggested.

Before the Gearheads could make up their minds, the scientists started talking.

"Tomorrow at this time, we'll be celebrating," one scientist said. "We will finally have the Rotting Fish Flower."

"Not many labs have one," another scientist said. "We might be the first in America." She pulled a large glass cylinder from her pack.

"If we can find it," a bearded scientist said. "I came searching five years ago and never found it."

"A hiker posted a picture on the Internet just last week," the first scientist said. "Unless another team beats us to it, tomorrow at sunrise, that specimen is ours."

Goldie tapped Li's and Val's shoulders. She motioned for them to follow her, and then she crawled quietly away from the scientists.

"They're going to steal the flower," Goldie said when they got back to the path.

"Is *steal* the right word?" Val asked.

"Whatever," Goldie said. "We need to get to it first. We need to go now." She stood and pointed to the top of the mountain.

"Shouldn't we wait until morning?" Li asked.

"No." Goldie started marching up the mountain.

"We should at least get Nacho and Ruby," Val said.

Goldie spun around. "Yes."

They went back and packed up their campsite. Goldie was disappointed that she wouldn't get a chance to try her campfire waffle iron. But smelling the flower was more important. She would not let Gran down.

"Does it still count as camping if I don't actually get to sleep?" Ruby asked. "I'd really like to cross camping off my life-goals list. And I'd really like never to go again."

"It counts," Goldie said.

They set off down the path. They tiptoed past the scientists' campsite and didn't turn on their flashlights until they were far away.

They marched up the mountain, only stopping for sips of water and to catch their breath.

After an hour, Ruby asked, "How much farther?"

"I'm sure it's close."

After two hours, Li gasped, "How much longer?"

"Around the next bend, I think."

After three hours, Val said, "I want to ask how much longer, but I have a feeling you don't know."

"The mountain must end eventually," Goldie said. "We're almost into the clouds."

The sun peeked over the horizon just as they reached the summit. They threw down their packs. Li, Val, and Ruby collapsed.

"Where's the flower?" Val asked. "I think I smell it."

"That could be me!" Li laughed. "I'm sweating all over. Even my eyeballs."

"Seriously, Gearheads. Where is it?" Goldie looked behind bushes and boulders. She checked the far side of trees. "There's no way the scientists beat us. Ruby, can you check the Internet? One scientist mentioned that a hiker posted a picture."

Ruby opened her minicomputer and set up the satellite dish. She tapped away. "Aha!" She showed the screen to Goldie.

The hiker stood over a plant no taller than her ankle. The flower was pink like a salmon.

"The flower is in bloom, and the sun is on the right side of the picture. That means it should be to the east. And that's Bloxtown on the left." Goldie scanned the area and figured out exactly where the hiker had been. "There!"

Goldie ran over. Li and Nacho followed right behind her. The petals of the flower were just opening as the sun inched higher in the sky.

Val stayed far away and held her nose. "Does it smell?"

"Not yet," Goldie answered.

Within a few minutes, the flower was in full bloom.

"It's beautiful," Goldie said, "but not stinky at all. I hope we have the right flower."

Val moved closer, squinting through her broken glasses. "It's pretty."

"I'm sure it's the right flower," Ruby called from behind them. "I'm reading about it right here. Pink petals with faint white stripes."

"Then this is it," Goldie said. She moved closer, taking a deep breath. Nothing.

Nacho circled the flower.

"Does this still count as finishing the dare?" Li asked. "I mean, it's not our fault it ran out of stink."

"I don't know," Goldie said, disappointed. She knelt right next to the flower and leaned in even closer.

"It says here," Ruby continued reading, "that the Rotting Fish Flower only smells when something blocks it from the sunlight. It acts like a skunk and . . ."

Goldie was only half listening to Ruby. Her focus was on the flower. She crept closer until her nose was only an inch away.

"No, Goldie!" Ruby yelled. "It's going to—"

The flower released a cloud of stink that surrounded Goldie, Li, Val, and Nacho.

Li coughed. His eyes bulged.

Val turned green.

Nacho rolled happily in the grass.

Goldie held a hand over her mouth and nose. "This is for you, Gran," she said.

The smell drifted over to Ruby. "Ewww!" She pulled a bottle of perfume from her suitcase and started spraying frantically.

"It's like a skunk died and then rolled in

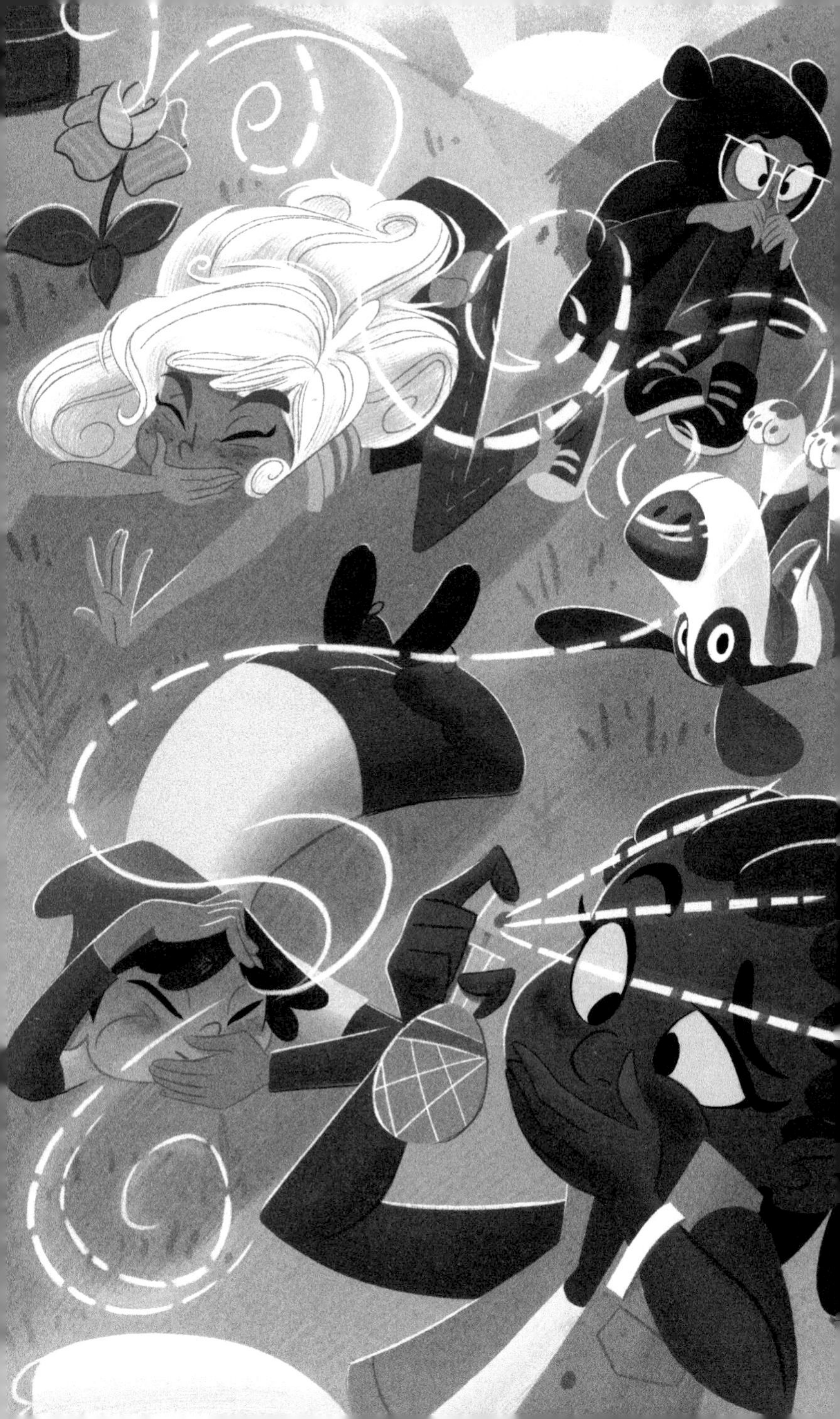

garbage," Li said.

"Then swam in a sewer and showered in sour milk," Goldie said.

"And then put on sweaty gym socks," Ruby added.

"That's a very active dead skunk," Val said, and they all laughed.

"Mission accomplished," Goldie said. "Now let's get out of here." They grabbed their packs and headed down the path.

Val dug in her pack as they walked. She pulled out clothespins. They put them on their noses. It didn't help much.

About a quarter of the way down, they met the scientists.

"Good morning." Goldie waved.

But the scientists couldn't answer. They

were too busy grabbing their noses. The bearded scientist bent over like he was going to be sick.

"You okay?" Goldie asked.

"You smell awful," one of the scientists said, gagging.

"Yeah, we do."

"Is it from the Rotting Fish Flower?" she asked.

"Yep." Goldie stepped closer, but the scientist waved her away. "And we don't even smell half as bad as the actual flower."

"The actual flower smells ten times worse," Val said.

The scientists looked at each other nervously as the Gearheads walked away.

"Maybe we shouldn't collect it," they heard one of the scientists say.

"I'm not going near that flower," said

another.

Goldie smiled at her friends. Not only had they checked a dare off the list, but they'd also saved the Rotting Fish Flower from ending up in a lab. It would remain on Rocky Point for all to enjoy.

Maybe enjoy *is not the right word,* Goldie thought.

TINY GOLDIE

It took Goldie seventeen showers to get rid of the smell of the Rotting Fish Flower. The stink still lingered on Nacho even after two dozen doggy baths. She suspected he might actually like the smell.

Goldie yawned. She could use a nap, but there wasn't time. They only had two days to finish the dares in Gran's book. She could sleep after she fulfilled her destiny.

She took the twirly slide from her bedroom to the BloxShop. The Gearheads had made plans to meet at two o'clock. Val and Ruby were waiting for her. Li, who lived in a house with a hundred clocks, was always late.

"Hey, Goldie," Ruby said. "I hope you don't mind, but I made a detailed plan for stealing the Bloxtown blueprints. Since we're breaking and entering, I want to make sure we don't get caught."

"I love a good plan," Goldie said with a smile.

"Have you ever seen a plan?" Val joked.

"No, but I've read about them in books." Goldie winked.

Goldie and Val took seats, and Ruby stood at the whiteboard.

"The Bloxtown Museum closes at six p.m.," Ruby began as Li came in and took a seat. "But it's not dark until eight. They have one security guard."

"How do you know all this?" Val asked.

"Internet research." Ruby held up her minicomputer. "The blueprints are in the *Early History of Bloxtown* exhibit."

"They're kept in Gran's original container, rolled up," Goldie said.

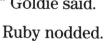

Ruby nodded. "Right. So we need to replace the tube with a fake." She pointed at Li. "Can you rappel from the ceiling, grab the blueprints, and replace them with a decoy?"

"Absolutely. They don't call me Li Gravity for nothing."

Val raised her hand.

"Go ahead, Val." Ruby pointed at her with a marker. "But you don't need to raise your hand."

"Has anyone considered just asking the museum for the blueprints?" Val asked.

"My Gran did years ago. And my dad asked again when I was little. They're not willing to share," Goldie replied.

"Val's got a point," Ruby said. "It's worth trying again before breaking in. Val, go make some calls."

Val rolled her eyes and saluted Ruby. "Yes, Captain Ruby." She left to use the house phone.

"Is that the whole plan?" Goldie asked. "Because if we need something with lasers and high-powered magnets, I can engineer that."

"No, that's not the whole plan." Ruby continued to talk. She made Li and Goldie memorize a map of the museum, including the positions of the air-conditioning ducts. She told them about the state-of-the-art alarm system that she was certain she could override with her minicomputer. And finally, she reminded them of the punishment if they got caught.

"I know we're minors," Ruby said. "But we could still end up in kid jail."

"Kid jail? Is that a thing?" Li asked.

"You don't want to find out," Ruby said. "Now, let's stick to the plan. Meet back here at seven. Wear all black. Not only is black in fashion this season, it's also the color of thieves."

"Gotcha, Captain Ruby," Li said. "I'm going to practice rappelling." He headed out the door.

"Do you have black overalls and a black T-shirt?" Ruby asked Goldie.

Goldie nodded. "I'm on it."

After Ruby had left, Goldie and Nacho got to work. First, she dyed some clothes black. Next, she made a fake blueprint tube that they would swap for the real one. Then she took out an invention she'd been playing with for weeks. She thought it might come in handy that night. She held it up for Nacho to see—and sniff.

"I call it Tiny Goldie."

Nacho gave it a lick. His slobbery tongue was as tall as the robot.

Goldie controlled Tiny Goldie by speaking into a remote control.

"Take three steps forward."

Tiny Goldie followed orders perfectly.

"Pick up the wrench."

Tiny Goldie did as she was told.

"Fly."

Tiny Goldie fell off the table, and her robot head popped off.

"I guess I should have given her wings if I wanted her to fly." Goldie got to work on the repairs.

As she screwed the head back on, Li

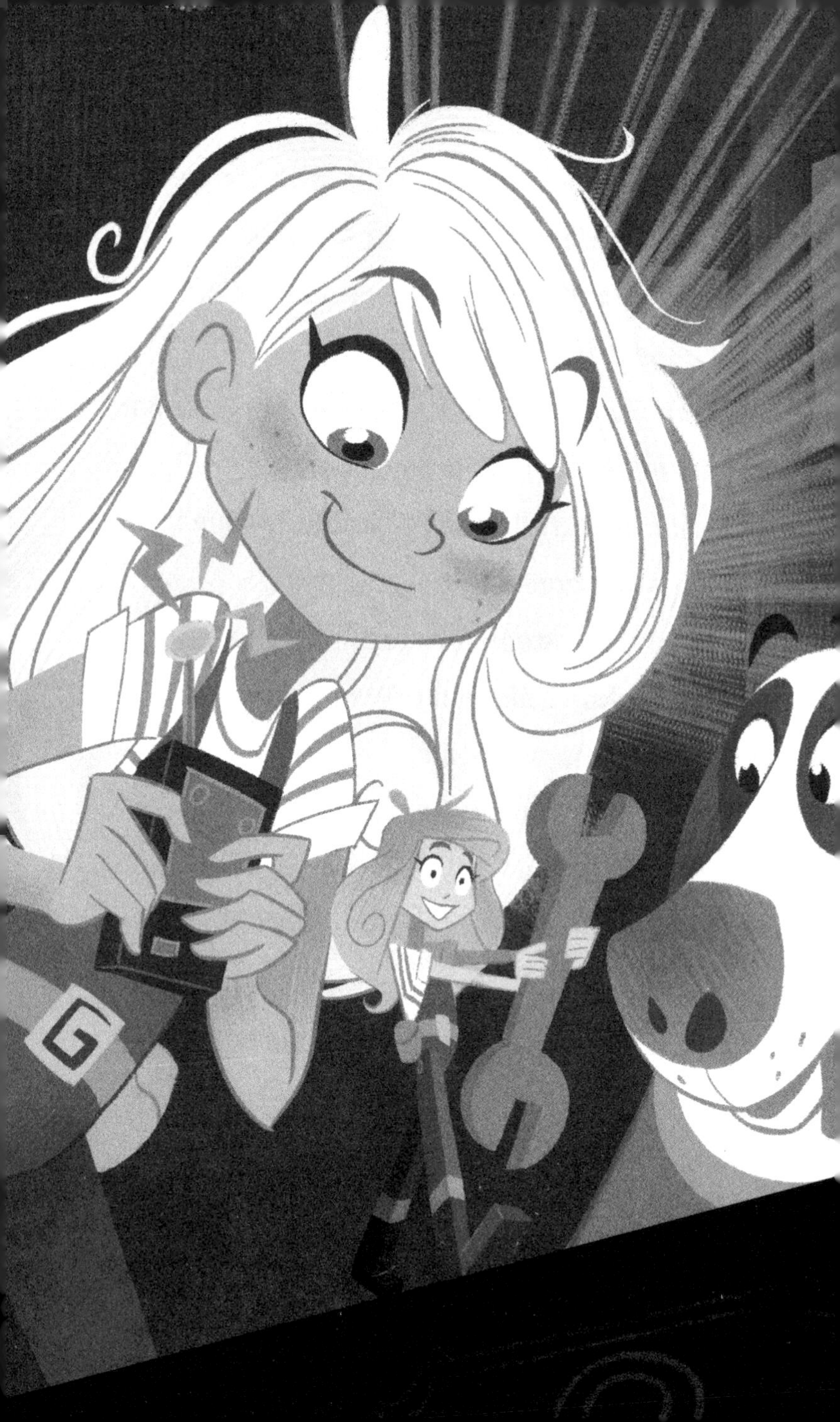

dropped silently from the ceiling. Goldie jumped when she saw him from the corner of her eye.

"Sweet, huh?" he said.

"Yeah," she agreed.

"Hey, G. I have no doubt we'll get these blueprints. We'll check off dare number ninety-nine. But we're not going to have a picnic on the moon. Not tomorrow, anyway. You know that, right? I don't want you to be disappointed."

"I can't believe my ears." Goldie pretended to clean them. "Is Li Gravity Zhang giving up before we've even tried?"

"But, G—"

"We *will* have a picnic on the moon," Goldie said. "I *will* live up to the Blox family name."

A WATCH-CROCODILE

That night Goldie and the Gearheads met outside the Bloxtown Museum. They wore all black, and Goldie carried a black duffel bag with her might-be-needed tools.

"Any luck asking for the blueprints?" Ruby whispered to Val.

"No. But they told me that Bloxtown magnets were on sale in the gift shop for ninety-nine cents."

"Thanks for trying," Goldie said.

Ruby took out her minicomputer. "In a few minutes, I'll have the alarm system deactivated. Then we go inside. On the second floor, we can crawl through the air ducts until we're over the exhibit. Then Li will rappel down and switch out the blueprints. We follow the same route out. The whole mission should take eleven minutes. We can't delay because the alarm will turn back on in twelve minutes."

"Should we sync our watches?" Goldie asked. She looked at her empty wrist. "Never mind."

Ruby tapped on the keyboard. "Three . . . two . . . one. The alarm system is down. Let's go."

"What about the guard?" Val asked.

"That's why we brought Nacho." Ruby patted the dog's head. "You're our watchdog. If you hear or smell anything, boy, let us know."

Goldie reached the front door first. She read the sign that warned of a state-of-the-art alarm system.

"Don't worry," Ruby said. "I promise. Their system is down."

Goldie put her hand on the door. No alarm. She pulled. Still no alarm or flashing lights. But the door didn't open either. "It's locked," she said.

Ruby tried pulling, too. Definitely locked. "It must have a manual lock."

"Did you bring your lock-picking machine?" Li asked Goldie.

"I've got something better." Goldie pulled out her little robot. "Meet Tiny Goldie."

"Isn't one of you enough?" Val joked.

"Not tonight." Goldie slid Tiny Goldie through the mail slot. She wished her luck.

Tiny Goldie parachuted to the ground.

Goldie pulled out the remote control to give the orders. "Unlock the door," she said.

Tiny Goldie walked across the entrance and went straight to the welcome desk.

"What is she doing?" Ruby asked.

Tiny Goldie jumped up and unlocked the door on a cabinet. Then she held her little robot arms in the air in victory.

"No," Goldie said. "Unlock the *front* door."

Tiny Goldie crossed the foyer again. She tossed a rope to the handle and climbed. She turned the lock, and the door opened.

"Yes!" the Gearheads cheered. They were in.

"Let's go," Ruby said. "The guard could be making his rounds and be here any second."

Goldie grabbed Tiny Goldie and followed the others down the hall. The stairs were in sight when Nacho suddenly stopped. His floppy ears stuck straight up.

"Hide!" Ruby whispered.

They all jumped into exhibits. Ruby and Goldie hid behind a small pyramid in Egypt. Val and Li squatted behind some columns in a Roman temple. Nacho cowered under a bench.

No one moved as the guard got closer.

Goldie heard the tapping of his shoes on the hard floor. She also heard scratching.

Goldie peeked around the pyramid. The guard was walking a crocodile on a leash. They had a *watchdog*, but he had a *watch-crocodile*. She glanced at her friends. Ruby looked like her eyes were about to pop out of her head.

The guard and the crocodile got closer. Goldie held her breath as they passed. Then the guard and his reptile partner were in front of Val and Li.

Keep moving, Goldie thought. *Keep moving*.

But the crocodile stopped and turned toward the Roman temple.

"What is it, Sweetness?" the guard asked his pet.

Goldie knew Val was nervous about getting caught. And she was probably terrified now about being bitten.

"We need to do something," Ruby said.

Goldie tried to reach quietly for Tiny Goldie. She loved her invention, but she loved her friends more. Before she could sacrifice Tiny Goldie, though, Sweetness suddenly turned away from Val and Li.

She was heading straight toward Nacho.

Ruby had to grab Goldie's arm to keep her from jumping out. "Look," she whispered.

Nacho had dropped a potato chip. Then another and another. He made a trail of snacks leading away from the Gearheads.

That's my dog, Goldie thought.

"What are you doing?" The guard yanked on the leash. "Sweetness, where are you going?"

The crocodile pulled the guard away.

Ruby popped out from her hiding spot. "We better hurry."

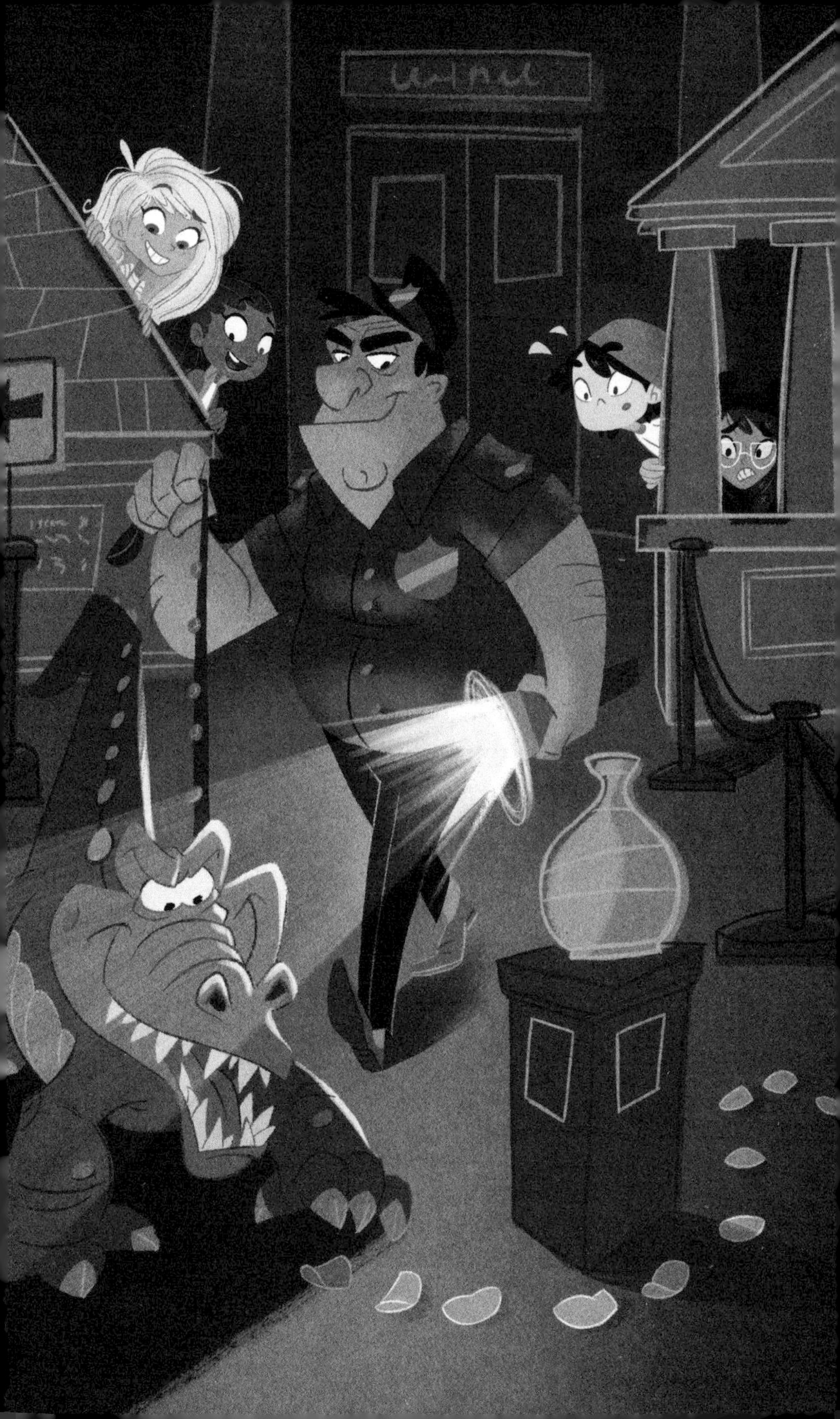

"Yeah," said Goldie, "before my dog becomes a doggy treat."

Ruby led them up the stairs to the second floor. She used her minicomputer to find the air duct. "There!"

Goldie took out a screwdriver and removed the metal cover. Li crawled in first.

"I'll keep an eye out," Val volunteered. She wedged the cover back in place and hid behind a sign.

Li, Ruby, and Goldie crawled until they were over the *Early History of Bloxtown* exhibit. Goldie used a micro saw to cut a hole in the ceiling. Li secured his ropes and put on his harness.

"Hurry," Ruby reminded him. "The alarms will turn back on in less than six minutes."

"Li Gravity out," he said as he dove through the hole. Ruby gasped, but Goldie knew better.

Li would have calculated everything perfectly. Doing physics calculations was his favorite hobby.

His ropes stopped him from hitting the floor with only an inch to spare. Li gave Goldie and Ruby a thumbs-up and a huge smile.

"Get the blueprints," Ruby whisper-yelled.

Li grabbed the tube. He secured it to his back.

"Where's the replacement?" Ruby asked Goldie. "Security might notice if it's missing. Especially after Val called asking about it."

"Here ya go." Goldie gave her the replica she'd made. It looked exactly like her grandmother's.

"I don't need it up here. Li needs it down there," Ruby said.

"On it," Goldie said. She gave the fake tube to Tiny Goldie.

Tiny Goldie rappelled down the line with one hand. She landed softly on Li's back and jumped to the ground. Li pointed to the spot for Tiny Goldie to place the decoy.

A tapping noise got Goldie's attention. It was Val. "Someone's coming," she whispered.

"Li, hurry. You're going to be caught." Goldie tugged the rope.

"But—"

"Come on!" Goldie yanked the rope again.

Li climbed up in seconds, but Tiny Goldie was left behind. The robot placed the decoy tube in the right place and hid behind Gran's old backpack.

Goldie saluted her little robot. "When you figure a way out, we'll meet you at the BloxShop." She replaced the ceiling cutout and quickly welded it back in place. The guard walked by the exhibit and didn't notice a thing.

"The alarm comes back on in three minutes," Ruby reminded them. "Move!"

They crawled out of the air duct and joined Val, then took off down the stairs. Nacho was napping at the bottom.

"How can you nap at a time like this?" Ruby asked him.

Nacho jumped up. The gang turned down the hall and almost ran into the back of the guard and his crocodile.

Li pulled them into a closet.

"What do we do?" Ruby asked.

Goldie looked in her duffel bag for something to get them out of this situation. She wished she had invented a sleeping gas that she could spray at the guard. But she had nothing that could help.

"We need a distraction," Li said. "One of us can run in one direction and lead the guard away. The rest of us can run out."

Nacho stepped forward to volunteer.

"But then how do we get you out?" Goldie asked her dog.

"Leave it to me," Val said. "I'll distract the guard. You guys run. I'll meet you outside."

"But, Val, you'll—" Ruby began.

"Trust me," Val interrupted.

"If she says she can do it, I believe her," Li said.

Val moved deeper into the museum. A second later, they heard a door slam. The guard heard it, too. He stopped and turned.

"This is our chance," Ruby said.

Li, Ruby, and Nacho ran toward the front door. Goldie paused and looked back toward Val. She couldn't leave her friend.

Goldie tiptoed after the guard, keeping a safe distance behind him. She watched as he approached Val, who was fake crying on a bench outside the restroom.

"Hey, what are you doing here?" the guard yelled. His watch-crocodile snapped its jaws.

Val looked up. "Thank goodness you found me! I must have fallen asleep. I was here on a field trip."

"You fell asleep?" the guard asked in disbelief. "How long have you been sleeping?"

Val shrugged. "I don't know. A few hours. It's still Thursday, right?"

"Yeah, still Thursday."

"Good." Val's eyes met Goldie's, and she flicked her head slightly like she was telling Goldie to get out.

"You're my hero," Val continued, speaking to the guard. "Can I borrow a phone to call my mom?"

Goldie snuck away. She knew Val wouldn't

really call her parents. She got out of the museum and met Ruby, Li, and Nacho beyond the parking lot.

Ruby gave her a hug. "Thank goodness. But I'm so worried about Val. Do you think she's been taken prisoner or eaten by the crocodile?"

"I wouldn't worry about Val. She's got skills," Goldie said.

Less than five minutes later, Val came walking over. "Looks like we accomplished another dare," she said.

EXCELLENT FOR ALL

Goldie pulled the cap off the blueprint tube. "I've been looking forward to this for—"

"Two days?" Val said.

"Technically, yes," Goldie replied. The Gearheads, Nacho, and Goldie's parents were gathered around her workbench.

"For the record," her mom said, "I do not approve of you stealing items from the museum. Or anywhere, for that matter."

"We have to insist that you return these blueprints," her dad added.

"You mean after we look at them, right?" Goldie asked. "It's not like the museum is open now."

"She has a point," her dad said.

Goldie gently removed the large rolled sheet of paper. She held her breath and slowly smoothed it out. Everyone inched closer.

Ruby held down one side, and Li held the other. Goldie rubbed her eyes.

Gran had signed her name and the date, so there was no doubt it was the right blueprint. Gran had drawn their house, the road, the pond, and the mountain, but there was nothing else except the words *Bloxtown: Excellent for All.*

"Looks like Gran wasn't much of a planner," Goldie said.

"I guess we know where you get it from," Val joked.

Goldie's dad scratched his head. "I bet she wanted this blueprint back so she could update it. Bloxtown has grown a lot since she started the town over forty years ago."

"Hey, look." Li lifted his corner. "There's something on the back."

Goldie flipped the sheet over. Gran's recipe for lime-chocolate-fig waffles was scribbled in the middle.

She tapped the recipe. "Or maybe she wanted this back. Shall we go to the kitchen?" Goldie licked her lips.

"It's late," her mom said. "I think it's time to say goodnight, Gearheads."

Her dad drove Ruby and Val home. Her mom went into the house. Li hung back.

"That's two dares, G. We did awesome," he said.

"And one to go." Goldie held up the book.

"But, G. We can't go to the moon. Not tomorrow, anyway. I've checked out the moon's orbit. Even if we had a rocket, it's not in the right position."

"Li, be positive. We'll figure it out. I'm not going to let my Gran down. And I want those waffles."

"But now you have the recipe. You can have them anytime."

"It's not the same." Goldie looked her oldest friend in the eye. "You're going to help me, right?" she asked.

Li sighed. "Definitely."

Goldie woke before the sun rose. She looked out her window. A sliver of moon hung in the sky.

"I'll see you soon." Goldie winked at the moon.

She poured a bowl of cereal and carried it to the BloxShop. She needed to get to work. Tiny Goldie sat on the workbench.

"You escaped!" Goldie gave her little robot a hug. "Good, because I'm going to need your help."

Goldie and Tiny Goldie started tinkering on a rocket. They had most of the supplies but were missing a key piece.

"Nacho, how much rocket fuel do we have?" Goldie asked.

Her dog carried over a plastic bottle.

"Not rocket fuel, boy," she said. "That's apple juice."

Later that morning, Li, Val, and Ruby came into the BloxShop. "How's it going, G?" Li asked.

"The rocket is coming along, but I don't have fuel or space suits or a picnic lunch. There's so much to do."

"We're here to help," Ruby said.

"Thanks, Gearheads." Goldie tried to sound

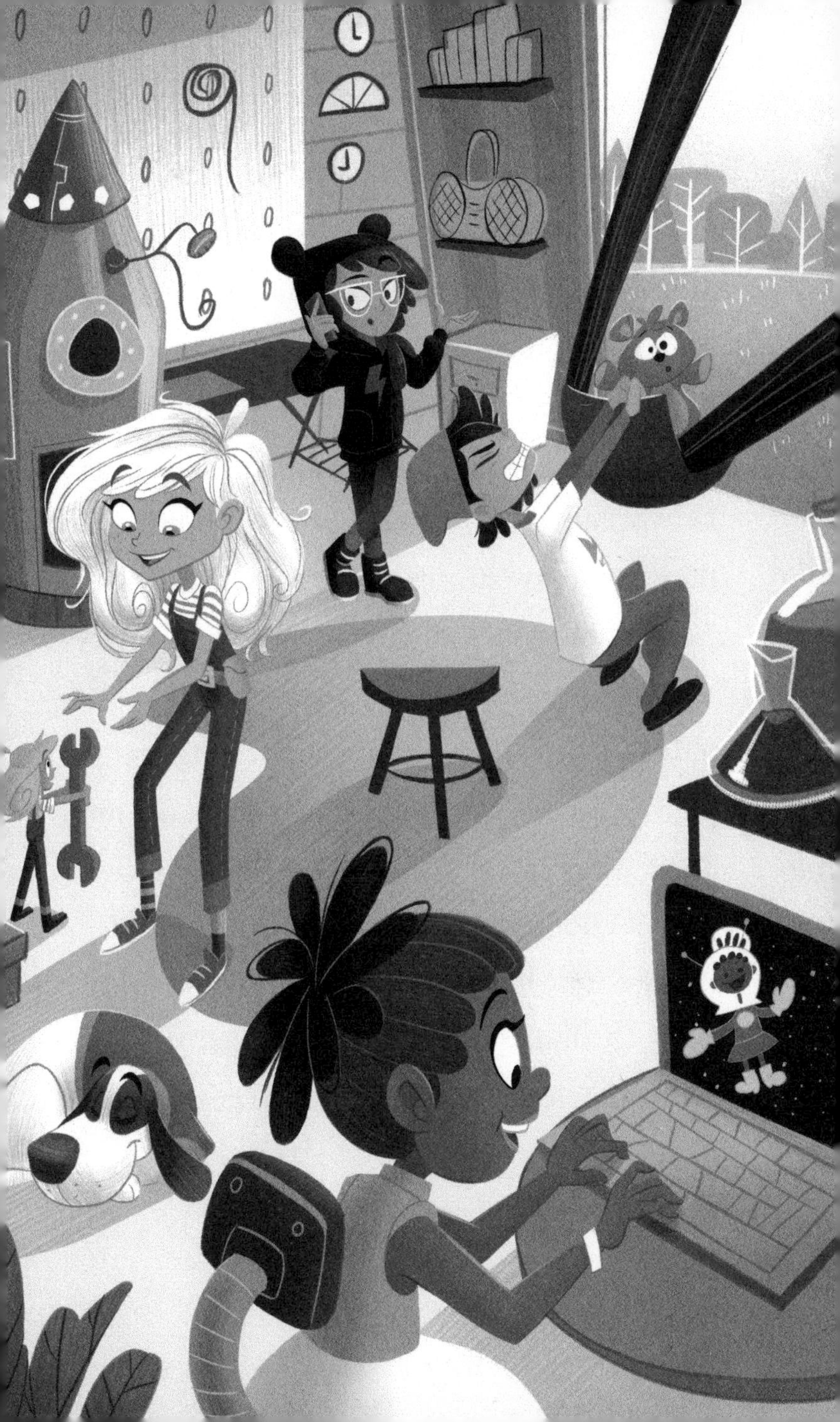

positive, but she was beginning to worry.

The Gearheads spent the rest of the morning trying every idea. They made a small rocket only big enough for one. Goldie tried to find fuel that would work, but nothing had the power she needed to leave Earth's atmosphere. Li worked on a slingshot, but it only flung things twenty stories high. Ruby worked on fashionable space suits. And Val called NASA.

"Excuse me, how much are four tickets to the moon?" Val asked. "For today's flights."

The space people were a bit rude and hung up on her.

"G, I don't think we can do this," Li said.

"We *will* have a picnic on the moon. I just need to think. I can engineer this!" Goldie's stomach felt heavy. She squeezed her eyes shut to keep from crying.

"Goldie—" began Li.

"Stop!" Goldie put her hands up and ran out of the BloxShop. She climbed the stairs to her room. When she got there, she locked the book.

"I'm sorry, Gran. I couldn't do it." She took her gran's red-and-white scarf and put it in a drawer. Then she flopped onto her bed. Nacho curled up next to her. He nudged her with his nose, but Goldie kept her head buried in her pillow.

T-MINUS TEN

Someone knocked on Goldie's door.

"I want to be alone, please," Goldie said.

"Okay," Val said without coming in.

A minute later, Li knocked on Goldie's window.

"Not now," she said. "I just need to be by myself."

He saluted and rode the zip line away.

Ruby sent Goldie a message on the computer, asking if she needed anything.

Goldie told her the same thing she'd told Li and Val.

Still, Goldie's brain kept running wild with ideas. She knew a picnic on the moon was impossible. But she couldn't turn off her creativity. She was daydreaming about a super-long ladder that telescoped as you climbed, when she heard banging.

Not banging, hammering.

Nacho ran to the window and looked out. His tail wagged.

Goldie followed him over. She caught a glimpse of Li carrying a helium tank across the yard. "What's going on?"

Goldie ran to the next window. Val was busy making modifications to Goldie's skateboard.

Goldie's jaw dropped. "Is Val engineering? That—that's incredible!" She was about to yell to Val, but Nacho nudged her toward her desk.

"If the Gearheads aren't giving up, neither am I." Goldie began drawing a new blueprint. A few minutes later, she crumpled it up. Then she made another. But that one, too, ended in a heap. Soon, Goldie was waist-deep in bad ideas.

"I only need one good idea," she said to Nacho.

Goldie kept working, brainstorming, and engineering. She knew her best idea wasn't always her first idea.

She was holding a T square and angle to a piece of paper when her computer beeped with an incoming message. She pressed the ACCEPT MESSAGE button. The screen came into focus.

"Hey, Goldie." Ruby's face filled the screen. "Can you do me a favor?"

"Sure," Goldie said.

"Can you give me a countdown? T-minus ten."

Goldie raised her eyebrows and wondered if Ruby was serious.

"Now, please," Ruby said. "We're on a deadline here."

"Okay. T-minus ten . . . nine . . . eight . . . seven . . ."

The screen flickered. Ruby was gone, and Goldie saw a rocket with BLOX EXPRESS painted on the side.

"Six . . . five . . . four . . ."

Smoke blew beneath the rocket. Goldie's stomach flipped with excitement.

"Three . . . two . . . one."

The rocket blasted off into the sky.

"Yes!" Goldie yelled. And the screen went black for a second.

"Ruby?" Goldie asked.

When the screen came back into focus, the Gearheads and Tiny Goldie were buckled into lawn chairs inside what looked like a space shuttle. The camera bounced.

"Hey, G," Li said with a salute. "Good news. We're on our way to the moon."

"And I packed a picnic." Val patted a basket strapped to another seat.

"We're going to finish the dares, Goldie," Ruby said. "And Tiny Goldie is here. She's representing the Blox family. You know, so it'll be official."

Tiny Goldie waved.

"You guys . . ." Goldie felt her throat tighten. "You're the best."

"We should be landing in a few minutes," Ruby explained. "The video may go out. But we're going to the moon, and we're going to have a picnic."

"We're going to finish the book," Li added.

Goldie gave them a thumbs-up. She had the best group of friends on earth, and the best on the moon. Even if they weren't really on the moon.

"Prepare for landing," Val said into her headset. The screen shook even more and then went black.

Nacho and Goldie waited. "Don't worry, boy. They'll be fine," Goldie said.

When the screen came back to life, the Gearheads wore stylish blue-and-green space suits. Ruby waved at Goldie.

"Wish you were here, G." Li pulled open the hatch door. He carried the camera in his hands. The focus was all over the place. One second Goldie was looking at his face. Then she saw the floor of the rocket, which looked a lot like the floor of the BloxShop.

"I feel like I'm there with you," Goldie said.

The Gearheads' camera looked out at the moon. The surface was like a gray giant blanket. Ruby stepped out first. She bounced across the ground.

"Wheee! The moon is so fun," Ruby said.

Val followed. She carried the picnic basket. Tiny Goldie floated behind, carrying a Blox family flag.

"What do you think?" Li asked Goldie through the camera lens.

"It's not like I imagined," Goldie said with a laugh. The sky was blue and had clouds.

"Um . . ." Li turned the camera back to his face. "The video is playing tricks on you." He fiddled with some knobs and the picture turned to black-and-white.

"Check out this crater!" Ruby yelled over her shoulder.

Goldie squinted at the screen. It looked like a kiddie pool filled with stones.

"And there you are." Ruby pointed. "On Earth." A huge sphere floated in the sky. Goldie knew it was a beach ball. *Pacific* was written across the ocean.

The Gearheads continued to bounce across the moon's surface. They smiled under their space helmets. When Val took out a red-and-white-checkered picnic blanket, it hovered because of the fake moon's low gravity.

That's impressive, Goldie thought. *They didn't miss anything. I wonder how they did that? A fan?*

Ruby helped Val stake the blanket to the moon's surface. Val opened the picnic basket, and a sandwich floated out. *Is that sandwich on a string?*

"How are you going to eat with helmets on?" Goldie asked.

"Be right back," Ruby said. Li cut the video. When it came back, Val and Ruby were rubbing their bellies like they'd just eaten.

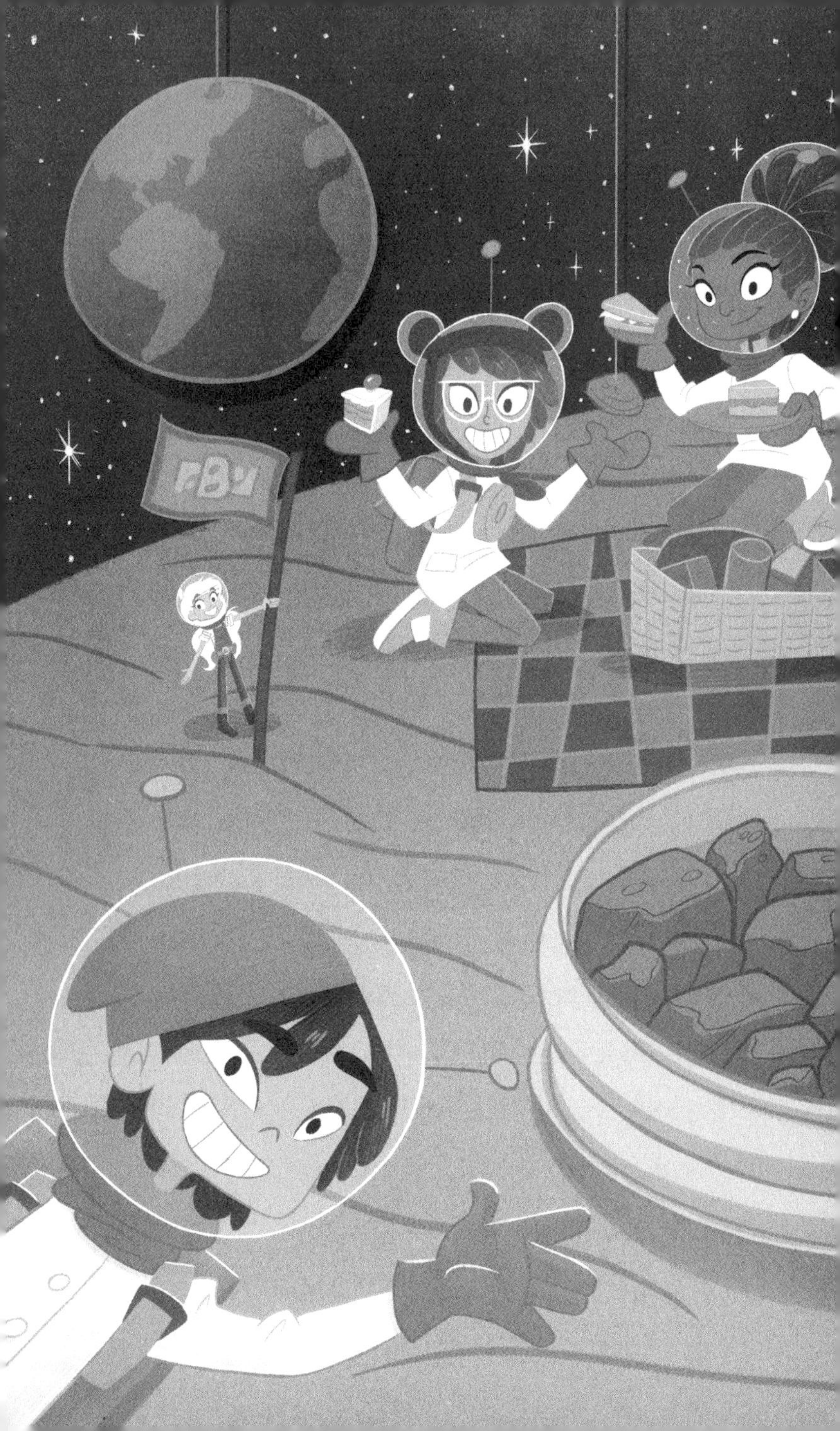

Goldie's stomach rumbled. She wanted to be there with her friends.

"So does this count?" Ruby asked Goldie. "Did we finish the book of dares?"

Goldie smiled and was about to say yes when another voice came through the video.

"Hey, kids." For a split second, the camera focused on Li's grandfather. He walked across the edge of the moon in flip-flops, shorts, and a Hawaiian shirt, with no space helmet. "What are you up to?" he asked.

"Turn off the camera!" Ruby yelled.

But instead, Li dropped the camera and ran across the bouncy surface, waving at his grandfather.

"You can't be on the moon!" he screamed. "Not without a helmet."

"Malfunction. Malfunction," Val repeated. "Signals crossed." She dove for the camera but missed. Her foot caught the edge of the gray blanket. Balloons rose from beneath, and the moon's surface slowly sank.

Tiny Goldie jumped onto a rising balloon. Her boot put a hole in it, and she shot across the yard. Ruby chased Tiny Goldie.

"I'll save you!" Ruby yelled. She jumped and landed on a trampoline. It sent her flying, and she bumped into the plastic Earth ball.

The ball crashed into the rocket, which was really Goldie's skateboard. It rolled full speed across the patio and freed the rest of the balloons.

The giant gray blanket flew over Val and wrapped her up like a cocoon. "Help!" she screamed. "I don't want to be a burrito."

The moon that the Gearheads had spent all day creating was destroyed in seconds. Li's grandfather stood watching with his mouth open.

Ruby and Li pulled off their helmets. Tiny Goldie pulled Val loose, and they removed their space gear, too.

Ruby looked sadly into the camera. "I'm sorry, Goldie. We tried, and we let you down."

GEORGE WASHINGTON'S NOSE

The Gearheads sat in the BloxShop. They weren't designing or engineering or planning. There were only a few hours left before the end of Gran's birthday, and they hadn't finished the dares.

"We tried to fake the last one, and we didn't even finish that," Ruby said. She sat with her head in her hands.

"You guys did a great job," Goldie said. "I can't believe you did all that for me."

"But we still failed," Val said.

"And I'm still hungry," Li said. "I could really go for a picnic. A big one."

"I wish the last dare was to have a picnic at the mall. That's only ten minutes away," Ruby said.

"Or at the park," Val said. "Or under an oak tree. Or near a lake. Or on the living room floor."

"Or on George Washington's nose," Li added.

"Huh?" Ruby asked.

"Mount Rushmore," Li said. "Not easy, but not as hard as getting to the moon."

"We need someplace in Bloxtown," Ruby said. "There are no presidential noses in Bloxtown, and there's no moon."

"Wait!" Goldie bolted out of her seat. "What did you say?"

Ruby gave her a strange look. "No

presidential noses or moon in Bloxtown?"

"You're right about the noses. But there is a moon. Repack the picnic basket. I'll be right back." Goldie climbed the rock wall out of the BloxShop and into the kitchen. She grabbed the box labeled STEAMED BROCCOLI from the freezer and a birthday candle from a drawer.

"Mom, Dad," Goldie called out. "I need a ride to the moon. Please."

Her dad stood in the doorway to the kitchen. "Are we taking the car, or do you have other plans?"

"The car will work."

Goldie, the Gearheads, Tiny Goldie, and Nacho piled into the backseat. Her mom drove, and her dad sat in the passenger seat.

"I'm going to need directions," her mom said as she backed out of the driveway.

"The moon," Goldie said. "You know where it is."

Her mom studied her in the rearview mirror. "I'm sorry, Goldie. I don't know what you're talking about."

"It's in the Milky Way," Goldie said.

"I know the moon is in our galaxy, but I—"

"The Milky Way," Li interrupted. "Brilliant, G!"

Val's and Ruby's faces lit up. They got it, too. But Goldie's parents didn't. They looked at each other and shrugged.

"The Milky Way Diner," Goldie explained. "The moon is there."

Her mom laughed. "Yes, it is."

Five minutes later, the car was parked in the lot. Val carried the picnic basket. Tiny Goldie clutched the small family flag. And

Goldie had Gran's lime-chocolate-fig waffles and the birthday candle.

The hostess greeted them at the door. She tried to seat them at the Jupiter table.

"No, the moon!" they all said.

Ruby and Tiny Goldie laid the picnic blanket across the moon table. Goldie asked the waitress to heat up the waffles.

"Please cover them in ice cream. And bring us every topping you have. And seven lemonades. And potato salad," Goldie ordered. "It's not a picnic without potato salad."

"Wait, we don't need potato salad," Val said. "I've got some. Enough to feed everyone on the moon." She pulled out three huge plastic containers.

Goldie picked up a fork. "Let the picnic begin!"

They ate most of Val's potato salad. Goldie's

dad told them that Gran used to put a secret ingredient in hers.

"Bacon?" Li asked.

Goldie's dad shook his head. "No. Gummy worms."

They laughed. When the waitress brought the waffles covered in ice cream, Goldie put a single candle on top. They lit it and sang "Happy Birthday" to Gran.

Val pulled out *The Big Book of Blox Dares*. "Should we check off the last dare?"

Goldie chewed and chewed her waffle. It was a bit tough but still good. Then she answered, "Definitely."

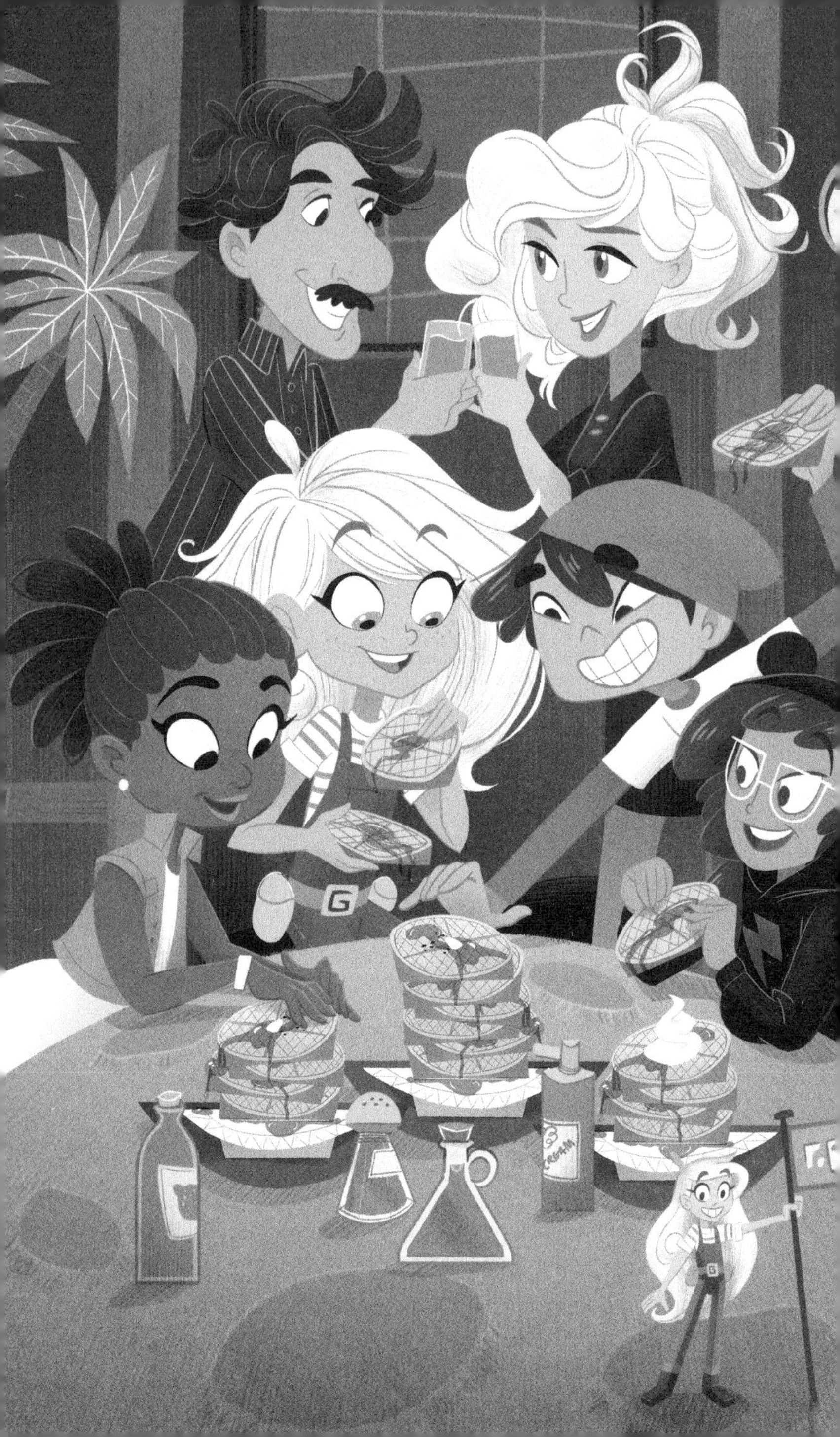
G
CREAM

I DARE YOU

Goldie's dad knocked on her bedroom door, and she let him in. She was dressed in her pajamas and ready to fall asleep.

"You've had a busy few days," he said.

"I feel like I could sleep for a year," she said.

They sat on her bed. Her dad had a present in his hand.

"This is for you," he said. "In honor of Gran's birthday."

Goldie took the gift and tore the paper off. It was a framed picture of Gran as a little girl.

One Goldie had never seen before. She wore the red-and-white scarf around her neck.

"Wow. She looks a lot like me. Or I look a lot like her," Goldie said.

"You do. But not only do you resemble each other. You are so much like her. Creative, hardworking, and fearless. She would be proud to call you her granddaughter."

"Thanks, Dad." Goldie hugged him around the waist.

"And, Goldie, I know that someday you will go to the moon. And probably even farther."

"I'd like to settle a town, like Gran did. Maybe New Bloxtown. On Venus."

Her dad kissed her forehead and said goodnight. Goldie dreamed of exploring outer space with the Gearheads. With her friends, anything was possible.

The next day, Goldie and the Gearheads met at the skateboard park. Goldie had her newly improved skateboard. She'd stenciled BLOX EXPRESS on the bottom. It had only one button—turbo. But it did have two safety features: a parachute and an air bag.

"Who wants to go first?" Goldie asked. To her surprise, both Li and Val volunteered.

"Val, wow! You want to try it?"

"Honestly, no." She shrugged. "But working on your Gran's dares was fun and exciting. So maybe I should try some other stuff."

"Yes!" Goldie cheered. Before Val could change her mind, Goldie strapped a helmet to her friend's head.

Li and Goldie led Val to the top of the ramp.

Ruby stayed on the ground with the camera ready.

"You got this, Val," Goldie said.

"Ride the skies," said Li, and slapped Val on the back. The impact sent Val down the ramp. She screamed the entire way and covered her eyes.

"Press the button, Val. Press it!" Goldie yelled. "I dare you."

Val opened her eyes. She bent low and put her arms out for balance. And then she pressed the button.

Val sailed up the next ramp and did a three-sixty at the top of the jump. She landed perfectly and rode the board back down.

"Whoa!" Li yelled. "That's going on the website."

Goldie, Li, and Ruby ran to Val's side.

"That was amazing!" Goldie said.

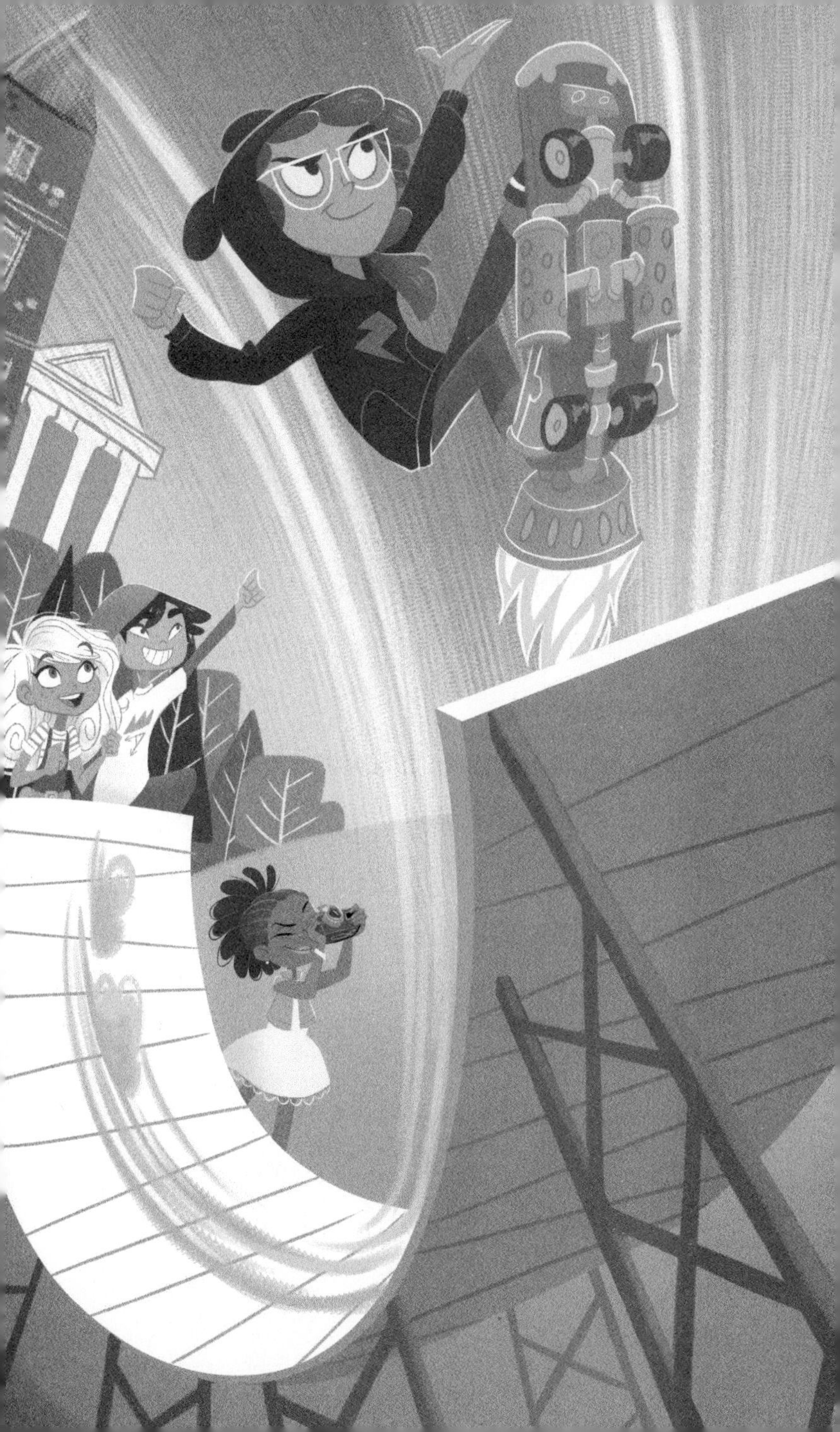

"Yeah, it was," Val said. Then she turned to Li. "When will my knees stop shaking?"

They all laughed.

"Do you want to try, Ruby?" Goldie asked.

"Is it a dare?" Ruby grinned.

Goldie shrugged. "Maybe it should be. Maybe we should have our own book. *The Gearheads' Big Book of Dares.*"

"Yes!" Li pumped his fist in the air. "I've got ten ideas already."

"Oh no," Val said. "If we're going to make a book of dares, we're all going to be the authors."

"I agree," Ruby said. "This is a group project."

"Let's do it," Goldie said.

They sat on a bench, and Goldie pulled out a notebook. They took turns passing it around, adding dare after dare. In a few minutes, they'd

filled an entire page.

"How do we decide which dare to do first?" Val asked.

"I can write a program that will decide for us," Ruby offered. She broke out her minicomputer.

Val read over the list. Her eyes grew wider. "Maybe we should do the ones least likely to kill us."

"We won't do anything dangerous," Goldie said.

"Not *too* dangerous," Li corrected her.

Ruby grabbed the notebook. "Got it! According to my random generator, our first dare will be . . ." She ran a finger down the notebook. "Jumping into a pool of vanilla ice cream."

"Yes!" Goldie cheered. "That's always been a dream of mine."

"At least I won't need a parachute," Val said.

"Just a life vest," Goldie said.

Val folded her arms. "How deep is this pool of ice cream?"

"You'll see." Goldie winked.